My Friend the Moon

VIKING KESTREL

Viking Penguin Inc., 40 West 23rd Street, New York, New York 10010, U.S.A.
Penguin Books Ltd, Harmondsworth, Middlesex, England
Penguin Books Australia Ltd, Ringwood, Victoria, Australia
Penguin Books Canada Limited, 2801 John Street, Markham, Ontario, Canada L3R 1B4
Penguin Books (N.Z.) Ltd, 182–190 Wairau Road, Auckland 10, New Zealand

Copyright © André Dahan, 1987
All rights reserved

First published in Switzerland as Mein Freund Der Mond *by Bohem Press, 1987.*
© 1987 by André Dahan.
This English language edition first published by Viking Penguin Inc., 1987
Published simultaneously in Canada

1 2 3 4 5 90 89 88 87

Library of Congress Catalog Card Number: 87-50063
ISBN 0-670-81569-1

My Friend the Moon

by André Dahan

Viking Kestrel

Why, hello, Moon.

I said, hello, Moon.

I just happened to be passing by.

What is that you're doing?

It looks like fun.

Uh, oh.

Splash!

Oh, my. Can you swim?

Thank goodness.

Let me help you.

Better now?

Come, we'll go to my house.

We're almost home.

My goodness, you're light as a feather.

Hmm. A tight fit.

But here we are.

Let's sing "Twinkle, twinkle little star."

This is fun!

Aren't you a _little_ tired?

I knew you'd like that one!

Mmm. I love chocolate pudding too.

It has been a busy night.

Why, hello, sun!

I can hardly believe our luck.